Beauty and the Beast

[original title page]

BEAUTY AND THE BEAST.

A TALE

FOR THE ENTERTAINMENT OF JUVENILE READERS.

Ornamented with Elegant Engravings.

First published 1756

Republished 2008 by Forgotten Books

www.forgottenbooks.org

PUBLISHER'S PREFACE

About the Book

"Beauty and the Beast (French: La Belle et la Bete) is a tradition-al fairy tale (type 425C -- search for a lost husband -- in the Aarne-Thompson classification). The first published version of the fairy tale was a meandering rendition by Madame Gabrielle-Suzanne Barbot de Villeneuve, published in La jeune americaine, et les contes marins in 1740. The best-known written version was an abridgement of Mme Villeneuve's work published in 1756 by Mme Jeanne-Marie Leprince de Beaumont, in Magasin des enfants, ou dialogues entre une sage gouvernante et plusieurs de ses elÃ¨ves; an English translation appeared in 1757.

Variants of the tale are known across Europe. In France, for example, Zemire et Azor is an operatic version of the story of Beauty and the Beast written by Marmontel and composed by Gretry in 1771. It had enormous success well into the 19th century. It is based on Mme Leprince de Beaumont's version of the tale."

(Quote from wikipedia.org)

About the Author

Jeanne Marie Le Prince de Beaumont (1711 - 1780)

Jeanne Marie Le Prince de Beaumont (born Rouen, France in 1711; died Chavanod, Savoie, in 1780) was a French novelist.

Her first work, a moralistic novel, The Triumph of Truth (le Triomphe de la Verite) was published in 1748.

She was first married in 1743, but this marriage was annulled after two years and in 1746 she left France to become a governess in London. She continued her literary career by publishing many school books (education complÃ¨te, ou Abrege de l'histoire universelle, 1762; le Mentor moderne, 1773). She then began to publish collections she called "magazines" of educational and moral stories and poems for children. She was among the first writers to specifically write fairy tales for children.

Over the next 30 years, dozens of versions of these "magazines" were printed, all containing the famous story Beauty and the Beast. Another famous storyteller of the era, Mme Gabrielle-Suzanne Barbot de Villeneuve, was the original author of the story; Le Prince de Beaumont used her basic theme and considerably revised and abridged the lengthy story. The success of the shorter version is why today Le Prince de Beaumont is usually known as the author. She also wrote other tales based on traditional fairy tale themes, such as Aurore and Aimee.

After a successful publishing career in England, she remarried, bore many children, and left England to live the rest of her life in Savoy.

CONTENTS

BEAUTY AND THE BEAST

THERE was once a very rich merchant, who had six children, three sons, and three daughters; being a man of sense, he spared no cost for their education, but gave them all kinds of masters. His daughters were extremely handsome, especially the youngest; when she was little, every body admired her, and called her *The little Beauty*; so that, as she grew up, she still went by the name of *Beauty*, which made her sisters very jealous. The youngest, as she was handsome, was also better than her sisters. The two eldest had a great deal of pride, because they were rich. They gave themselves ridiculous airs, and would not visit other merchants' daughters, nor keep company with any but persons of quality. They went out every day upon parties of pleasure, balls, plays, concerts, etc. and laughed at their youngest sister, because she spent the greatest part of her time in reading good books. As it was known that they were to have great fortunes, several eminent merchants made their addresses to them; but the two eldest said they would never marry, unless they could meet with a Duke, or an Earl at least. Beauty very civilly thanked them that courted her, and told them she was too young yet to marry, but chose to stay with her father a few years longer.

All at once the merchant lost his whole fortune, excepting a small country-house at a great distance from town, and told his children, with tears in his eyes, they most go there and work for their living. The two eldest answered, that they would not leave the town, for they had several lovers, who they were sure would be glad to have them, though they had no fortune; but in this they were mistaken, for their lovers slighted and forsook them in their poverty. As they were not beloved on account of their pride, every body said, "they do not deserve to be pitied, we are glad to see their pride humbled, let them go and give themselves quality airs in milking the cows and minding their dairy. But, (added they,) we are extremely concerned for Beauty, she was such a charming, sweet-tempered creature, spoke so kindly to poor people, and was of such an affable, obliging disposition." Nay, several gentlemen would have married her, though they knew she had not a penny; but she told them she could not think of leaving her poor father in his misfortunes, but was determined to go along with him into the country to comfort and attend him. Poor Beauty at first was sadly grieved at the loss of her fortune; "but, (she said to herself,) were I to cry ever so much, that would not make things better, I must try to make myself happy without a fortune." When they came to their country-house, the merchant and his three sons applied themselves to husbandry and tillage; and Beauty rose at four in the morning, and made haste to have the house clean, and breakfast ready for the family. In the beginning she found it very difficult, for she had not been used to work as a servant; but in less than two months she grew stronger and healthier than ever. After she had done her work, she read, played on the harpsichord, or else sung whilst she spun. On the contrary, her two sisters did not know how to spend their time; they got up at ten, and did nothing but saunter about the whole day, lamenting the loss of their fine clothes and acquaintance. "Do but see our youngest sister, (said they one to the other,) what a poor, stupid mean-spirited creature she is, to be contented with such an unhappy situation." The good merchant was of a quite different opinion; he knew very well that Beauty out-shone her sisters, in her person as well as her mind, and admired her humility, industry, and patience; for her sisters not only left her all the work of the house to do, but insulted her every moment.

The family had lived about a year in this retirement, when the merchant received a letter, with an account that a vessel, on board of which he had effects, was safely arrived. This news had liked to have turned the heads of the two eldest daughters, who immediately flattered themselves with the hopes of returning to town; for they were quite weary of a country life; and when they saw their father ready to set out, they begged of him to buy them new gowns, caps, rings, and all manner of trifles; but Beauty asked for nothing, for she thought to herself, that all the money her father was going to receive would scarce be sufficient to purchase every thing her sisters wanted. "What will you have, Beauty?" said her father. "Since you are so kind as to think of me, (answered she,) be so kind as to bring me a rose, for as none grow hereabouts, they are a kind of rarity." Not that Beauty cared for a rose, but she asked for something, lest she should seem by her example to condemn her sisters' conduct, who would have said she did it only to look particular. The good man went on his journey; but when he came there, they went to law with him about the merchandize, and after a great deal of trouble and pains to no purpose, he came back as poor as before.

He was within thirty miles of his own house, thinking on the pleasure he should have in seeing his children again, when going through a large forest he lost himself. It rained and snowed terribly, besides, the wind was so high, that it threw him twice off his horse; and night coming on, he began to apprehend being either starved to death with cold and hunger, or else devoured by the wolves, whom he heard howling all around him, when, on a sudden, looking through a long walk of trees, he saw a light at some distance, and going on a little farther, perceived it came from a palace illuminated from top to bottom. The merchant returned God thanks for this happy discovery, and hasted to the palace; but was greatly surprised at not meeting with anyone in the out-courts. His horse followed him, and seeing a large stable open, went in, and finding both hay and oats, the poor beast, who was almost famished, fell to eating very heartily. The merchant tied him up to the manger, and walked towards the house, where he saw no one, but entering into a large hall, he found a good fire, and a table plentifully set out, with but one cover laid. As he was wet quite through with the rain and snow, he drew near the fire to dry himself. "I hope, (said he,) the master of the house, or his servants, will excuse the liberty I take; I suppose it will not be long before some of them appear."

He waited a considerable time, till it struck eleven, and still nobody came: at last he was so hungry that he could stay no longer, but took a chicken and ate it in two mouthfuls, trembling all the while. After this, he drank a few glasses of wine, and growing more courageous, he went out of the hall, and crossed through several grand apartments with magnificent furniture, till he came into a chamber, which had an exceeding good bed in it, and as he was very much fatigued, and it was past midnight, he concluded it was best to shut the door, and go to bed.

It was ten the next morning before the merchant waked, and as he was going to rise, he was astonished to see a good suit of clothes in the room of his own, which were quite spoiled. "Certainly, (said he,) this palace belongs to some kind fairy, who has seen and pitied my distress." He looked through a window, but instead of snow saw the most delightful arbours, interwoven with the most beautiful flowers that ever were beheld. He then returned to the great hall, where he had supped the night before, and found some chocolate ready made on a little table. "Thank you, good Madam Fairy, (said he aloud,) for being so careful as to provide me a breakfast; I am extremely obliged to you for all your favours."

The good man drank his chocolate, and then went to look for his horse; but passing through an arbour of roses, he remembered Beauty's request to him, and gathered a branch on which were several; immediately he heard a great noise, and saw such a frightful beast coming towards him, that he was ready to faint away. "You are very ungrateful, (said the beast to him, in a terrible voice) I have saved your life by receiving you into my castle, and, in return, you steal my roses, which I value beyond any thing in the universe; but you shall die for it; I give you but a quarter of an hour to prepare yourself, to say your prayers." The merchant fell on his knees, and lifted up both his hands: "My Lord (said he,) I beseech you to forgive me, indeed I had no intention to offend in gathering a rose for one of my daughters, who desired me to bring her one." "My name is not My Lord, (replied the monster,) but Beast; I don't love compliments, not I; I like people should speak as they think; and so do not imagine I am to be moved by any of your flattering speeches; but you say you have got daughters; I will forgive you, on condition that one of them come willingly, and suffer for you. Let me have no words, but go about your business, and swear that if your daughter refuse to die in your stead, you will return within three months." The merchant had no mind to sacrifice his daughters to the ugly monster, but he thought, in obtaining this respite, he should have the satisfaction of seeing them once more; so he promised upon oath, he would return, and the Beast told him he might set out when he pleased; "but, (added he,) you shall not depart empty handed; go back to the room where you lay, and you will see a great empty chest; fill it with whatever you like best, and I will send it to your home," and at the same time Beast withdrew. "Well (said the good man to himself) if I must die, I shall have the comfort, at least, of leaving something to my poor children."

He returned to the bed-chamber, and finding a great quantity of broad pieces of gold, he filled the great chest the Beast had mentioned, locked it, and afterwards took his horse out of the stable, leaving the palace with as much grief as he had entered it with joy. The horse, of his own accord, took one of the roads of the forest; and in a few hours the good man was at home. His children came around him, but, instead of receiving their embraces with pleasure, he looked on them, and, holding up the branch he had in his hands, he burst into tears. "Here, Beauty, (said he,) take these roses; but little do you think how dear they are like to cost your unhappy father; and then related his fatal adventure: immediately the two eldest set up lamentable outcries, and said all manner of ill-natured things to Beauty, who did not cry at all. "Do but see the pride of that little wretch, (said they); she would not ask for fine clothes, as we did; but no, truly, Miss wanted to distinguish herself; so now she will be the death of our poor father, and yet she does not so much as shed a tear." "Why should I, (answered Beauty,) it would be very needless, for my father shall not suffer upon my account, since the monster will accept of one of his daughters, I will deliver myself up to all his fury, and I am very happy in thinking that my death will save my father's life, and be a proof of my tender love for him." "No, sister, (said her three brothers,) that shall not be, we will go find the monster, and either kill him, or perish in the attempt." "Do not imagine any such thing, my sons, (said the merchant,) Beast's power is so great, that I have no hopes of your overcoming him; I am charmed with Beauty's kind and generous offer, but I cannot yield to it; I am old, and have not long to live, so can only lose a few years, which I regret for your sakes alone, my dear children." "Indeed, father (said Beauty), you shall not go to the palace without me, you cannot hinder me from following you." It was to no purpose all they could say, Beauty still insisted on setting out for the fine palace; and her sisters were delighted at it, for her virtue and amiable qualities made them envious and jealous.

The merchant was so afflicted at the thoughts of losing his daughter, that he had quite forgot the chest full of gold; but at night, when he retired to rest, no sooner had he shut his chamber-door, than, to his great astonishment, he found it by his bedside; he was determined, however, not to tell his children that he was grown rich, because they would have wanted to return to town, and he was resolved not to leave the country; but he trusted Beauty with the secret: who informed him, that two gentlemen came in his absence, and courted her sisters; she begged her father to consent to their marriage, and give them fortunes; for she was so good, that she loved them, and forgave them heartily all their ill-usage. These wicked creatures rubbed their eyes with an onion, to force some tears when they parted with their sister; but her brothers were really concerned. Beauty was the only one who did not shed tears at parting, because she would not increase their uneasiness.

The horse took the direct road to the palace; and towards evening they perceived it illuminated as at first: the horse went of himself into the stable, and the good man and his daughter came into the great hall, where they found a table splendidly served up, and two covers. The merchant had no heart to eat; but Beauty endeavoured to appear cheerful, sat down to table, and helped him. Afterwards, thought she to herself, "Beast surely has a mind to fatten me before he eats me, since he provides such a plentiful entertainment." When they had supped, they heard a great noise, and the merchant, all in tears, bid his poor child farewell, for he thought Beast was coming. Beauty was sadly terrified at his horrid form, but she took courage as well as she could, and the monster having asked her if she came willingly; "y--e--s," said she, trembling. "You are very good, and I am greatly obliged to you; honest man, go your ways tomorrow morning, but never think of returning here again. Farewell, Beauty." "Farewell, Beast," answered she; and immediately the monster withdrew. "Oh, daughter, (said the merchant, embracing Beauty,) I am almost frightened to death; believe me, you had better go back, and let me stay here." "No, father, (said Beauty, in a resolute tone,) you shall set out tomorrow morning, and leave me to the care and protection of Providence." They went to bed, and thought they should not close their eyes all night; but scarce were they laid down, than they fell fast asleep; and Beauty dreamed, a fine lady came, and said to her, "I am content, Beauty, with your good will; this good action of yours, in giving up your own life to save your father's, shall not go unrewarded." Beauty waked, and told her father her dream, and though it helped to comfort him a little, yet he could not help crying bitterly, when he took leave of his dear child.

As soon as he was gone, Beauty sat down in the great hall, and fell a crying likewise; but as she was mistress of a great deal of resolution, she recommended herself to God, and resolved not to be uneasy the little time she had to live; for she firmly believed Beast would eat her up that night.

However, she thought she might as well walk about till then, and view this fine castle, which she could not help admiring; it was a delightful pleasant place, and she was extremely surprised at seeing a door, over which was wrote, "BEAUTY'S APARTMENT." She opened it hastily, and was quite dazzled with the magnificence that reigned throughout; but what chiefly took up her attention, was a large library, a harpsichord, and several music books. "Well, (said she to herself,) I see they will not let my time hang heavy on my hands for want of amuse-ment." Then she reflected, "Were I but to stay here a day, there would not have been all these preparations." This consideration inspired her with fresh courage; and opening the library, she took a book, and read these words in letters of gold:--

"Welcome, Beauty, banish fear, You are queen and mistress here; Speak your wishes, speak your will, Swift obedience meets them still."

"Alas, (said she, with a sigh,) there is nothing I desire so much as to see my poor father, and to know what he is doing." She had no sooner said this, when casting her eyes on a great looking-glass, to her great amazement she saw her own home, where her father arrived with a very dejected countenance; her sisters went to meet him, and, notwithstanding their endeavours to appear sorrowful, their joy, felt for having got rid of their sister, was visible in every feature: a moment after, every thing disappeared, and Beauty's apprehensions at this proof of Beast's complaisance.

At noon she found dinner ready, and while at table, was entertained with an excellent concert of music, though without seeing any body: but at night, as she was going to sit down to supper, she heard the noise Beast made; and could not help being sadly terrified. "Beauty, (said the monster,) will you give me leave to see you sup?" "That is as you please," answered Beauty, trembling. "No, (replied the Beast,) you alone are mistress here; you need only bid me be gone, if my presence is troublesome, and I will immediately withdraw: but tell me, do not you think me very ugly?" "That is true, (said Beauty,) for I cannot tell a lie; but I believe you are very good-natured." "So I am, (said the monster,) but then, besides my ugliness, I have no sense; I know very well that I am a poor, silly, stupid creature." "'Tis no sign of folly to think so, (replied Beauty,) for never did fool know this, or had so humble a conceit of his own under-standing." "Eat then, Beauty, (said the monster,) and endeavour to amuse yourself in your palace; for every thing here is yours, and I should be very uneasy if you were not happy." "You are very obliging, (answered Beauty;) I own I am pleased with your kindness, and when I consider that, your deformity scarce appears." "Yes, yes, (said the Beast,) my heart is good, but still I am a monster." "Among mankind, (says Beauty,) there are many that deserve that name more than you, and I prefer you, just as your are, to those, who, under a human form, hide a treacherous, corrupt, and ungrateful heart." "If I had sense enough, (replied the Beast,) I would make a fine compliment to thank you, but I am so dull, that I can only say, I am greatly obliged to you." Beauty ate a hearty supper, and had almost conquered her dread of the monster; but she had liked to have fainted away, when he said to her, "Beauty, will you be my wife?" She was some time before she durst answer; for she was afraid of making him angry, if she refused. At last, however, she said, trembling, "No, Beast." Immediately the poor monster began to sigh, and hissed so frightfully, that the whole palace echoed. But Beauty soon recovered her fright, for Beast having said, in a mournful voice, "then farewell, Beauty," left the room; and only turned back, now and then, to look at her as he went out.

When Beauty was alone, she felt a great deal of compassion for poor Beast. "Alas, (said she,) 'tis a thousand pities any thing so good- natured should be so ugly."

Beauty spent three months very contentedly in the palace: every evening Beast paid her a visit, and talked to her during supper, very rationally, with plain good common sense, but never with what the world calls wit; and Beauty daily discovered some valuable qualifications in the monster; and seeing him often, had so accustomed her to his deformity, that, far from dreading the time of his visit, she would often look on her watch to see when it would be nine; for the Beast never missed coming at that hour. There was but one thing that gave Beauty any concern, which was, that every night, before she went to bed, the monster always asked her, if she would be his wife.

One day she said to him, "Beast, you make me very uneasy, I wish I could consent to marry you, but I am too sincere to make you believe that will ever happen: I shall always esteem you as a friend; endeavour to be satisfied with this." "I must, said the Beast, for, alas! I know too well my own misfortune; but then I love you with the tenderest affection: however, I ought to think myself happy that you will stay here; promise me never to leave me." Beauty blushed at these words; she had seen in her glass, that her father had pined himself sick for the loss of her, and she longed to see him again. "I could, (answered she), indeed promise never to leave you entirely, but I have so great a desire to see my father, that I shall fret to death, if you refuse me that satisfaction." "I had rather die myself, (said the monster,) than give you the least uneasiness: I will send you to your father, you shall remain with him, and poor Beast will die with grief." "No, (said Beauty, weeping,) I love you too well to be the cause of your death: I give you my promise to return in a week: you have shewn me that my sisters are married, and my brothers gone to the army; only let me stay a week with my father, as he is alone." "You shall be there tomorrow morning, (said the Beast,) but remember your promise: you need only lay your ring on the table before you go to bed, when you have a mind to come back: farewell, Beauty." Beast sighed as usual, bidding her good night; and Beauty went to bed very sad at seeing him so afflicted. When she waked the next morning, she found herself at her father's, and having rang a little bell, that was by her bedside, she saw the maid come; who, the moment she saw her, gave a loud shriek; at which the good man ran up stairs, and thought he should have died with joy to see his dear daughter again. He held her fast locked in his arms above a quarter of an hour. As soon as the first transports were over, Beauty began to think of rising, and was afraid she had no clothes to put on; but the maid told her, that she had just found, in the next room, a large trunk full of gowns, covered with gold and diamonds.

Beauty thanked good Beast for his kind care, and taking one of the plainest of them, she intended to make a present of the others to her sisters. She scarce had said so, when the trunk disappeared. Her father told her, that Beast insisted on her keeping them herself; and immediately both gowns and trunk came back again.

Beauty dressed herself; and in the mean time they sent to her sisters, who hasted thither with their husbands. They were both of them very unhappy. The eldest had married a gentleman, extremely handsome indeed, but so fond of his own person, that he was full of nothing but his own dear self, and neglected his wife. The second had married a man of wit, but he only made use of it to plague and torment every body, and his wife most of all. Beauty's sisters sickened with envy, when they saw her dressed like a Princess, and more beautiful than ever; nor could all her obliging affectionate behaviour stifle their jealousy, which was ready to burst when she told them how happy she was. They went down into the garden to vent it in tears; and said one to the other, "In what is this little creature better than us, that she should be so much happier?" "Sister, said the eldest, a thought just strikes my mind; let us endeavour to detain her above a week, and perhaps the silly monster will be so enraged at her for breaking her word, that he will devour her." "Right, sister, answered the other, therefore we must shew her as much kindness as possible." After they had taken this resolution, they went up, and behaved so affectionately to their sister, that poor Beauty wept for joy. When the week was expired, they cried and tore their hair, and seemed so sorry to part with her, that she promised to stay a week longer.

In the mean time, Beauty could not help reflecting on herself for the uneasiness she was likely to cause poor Beast, whom she sincerely loved, and really longed to see again. The tenth night she spent at her father's, she dreamed she was in the palace garden, and that she saw Beast extended on the grass-plot, who seemed just expiring, and, in a dying voice, reproached her with her ingratitude. Beauty started out of her sleep and bursting into tears, "Am not I very wicked, (said she) to act so unkindly to Beast, that has studied so much to please me in every thing? Is it his fault that he is so ugly, and has so little sense? He is kind and good, and that is sufficient. Why did I refuse to marry him? I should be happier with the monster than my sisters are with their husbands; it is neither wit nor a fine person in a husband, that makes a woman happy; but virtue, sweetness of temper, and complaisance: and Beast has all these valuable qualifications. It is true, I do not feel the tenderness of affection for him, but I find I have the highest gratitude, esteem, and friendship; and I will not make him miserable; were I to be so ungrateful, I should never forgive myself." Beauty having said this, rose, put her ring on the table, and then laid down again; scarce was she in bed before she fell asleep; and when she waked the next morning, she was overjoyed to find herself in the Beast's palace. She put on one of her richest suits to please him, and waited for evening with the utmost impatience; at last the wished-for hour came, the clock struck nine, yet no Beast appeared. Beauty then feared she had been the cause of his death; she ran crying and wringing her hands all about the palace, like one in despair; after having sought for him every where, she recollected her dream, and flew to the canal in the garden, where she dreamed she saw him. There she found poor Beast stretched out, quite senseless, and, as she imagined, dead. She threw herself upon him without any dread, and finding his heart beat still, she fetched some water from the canal, and poured it on his head. Beast opened his eyes, and said to Beauty, "You forgot your promise, and I was so afflicted for having lost you, that I resolved to starve myself; but since I have the happiness of seeing you once more, I die satisfied." "No, dear Beast, (said Beauty,) you must not die; live to be my husband; from this moment I give you my hand, and swear to be none but yours. Alas! I thought I had only a friendship for you, but, the grief I now feel convinces me, that I cannot live without you." Beauty scarcely had pronounced these words, when she saw the palace sparkle with light; and fireworks, instruments of music, every thing, seemed to give notice of some great event: but nothing could fix her attention; she turned to her dear Beast, for whom she trembled with fear; but how great was her surprise! Beast had disappeared, and she saw, at her feet, one of the loveliest Princes that eye ever beheld, who returned her thanks for having put an end to the charm, under which he had so long resembled a Beast. Though this Prince was worthy of all her attention, she could not forbear asking where Beast was. "You see him at your feet, (said the Prince): a wicked fairy had condemned me to remain under that shape till a beautiful virgin should consent to marry me: the fairy likewise enjoined me to conceal my understanding; there was only you in the world generous enough to be won by the goodness of my temper; and in offering you my crown, I can't discharge the obligations I have to you." Beauty, agreeably surprised, gave the charming Prince her hand to rise; they went together into the castle, and Beauty was overjoyed to find, in the great hall, her father and his whole family, whom the beautiful lady, that appeared to her in her dream, had conveyed thither.

"Beauty, (said this lady,) come and receive the reward of your judicious choice; you have preferred virtue before either wit or beauty, and deserve to find a person in whom all these qualifications are united: you are going to be a great Queen; I hope the throne will not lessen your virtue, or make you forget yourself. As to you, ladies, (said the Fairy to Beauty's two sisters,) I know your hearts, and all the malice they contain: become two statues; but, under this transformation, still retain your reason. You shall stand before your sister's palace gate, and be it your punishment to behold her happiness; and it will not be in your power to return to your former state till you own your faults; but I am very much afraid that you will always remain statues. Pride, anger, gluttony, and idleness, are sometimes conquered, but the conversion of a malicious and envious mind is a kind of miracle." Immediately the fairy gave a stroke with her wand, and in a moment all that were in the hall were transported into the Prince's palace. His subjects received him with joy; he married Beauty, and lived with her many years; and their happiness, as it was founded on virtue, was complete.

Read these similar books for free at forgottenbooks.org:

Grimm's Fairy Tales

The Hound of the Baskervilles

A True Story

The Dramas of Euripides

The Works of Lucian of Samosata

The Alchemist

The Satyricon of Petronius

Dorothy and the Wizard in Oz

Read or order online at:

www.forgottenbooks.org
or
www.amazon.com

Made in the USA